Jasper's **SUPER** STUPENDOUS **FORT** of AWESOMENESS!

For my friends

Copyright © 2020 by Alex Willan
All rights reserved. Published in the United States by Doubleday, an imprint of
Random House Children's Books, a division of Penguin Random House LLC, New York.
Doubleday and the colophon are registered trademarks of Penguin Random House LLC.
Visit us on the Web! rhcbooks.com
Educators and librarians, for a variety of teaching tools, visit us at RHTeachersLibrarians.com
Library of Congress Cataloging-in-Publication Data
Names: Willan, Alex, author, illustrator.
Title: Jasper & Ollie build a fort / Alex Willan.
Other titles: Jasper and Ollie build a fort
Description: First edition. | New York : Doubleday Books for Young Readers, [2020] |
Series: Jasper & Ollie | Audience: Ages 3–6.
Summary: Jasper the fox and Ollie the sloth have a fort-building contest in their yard.
—Provided by publisher.
Identifiers: LCCN 2019027878 (print) | LCCN 2019027879 (ebook) |
ISBN 978-0-525-64524-5 (hc) | ISBN 978-0-525-64527-6 (library binding) |
ISBN 978-0-525-64526-9 (ebook)
Subjects: CYAC: Foxes—Fiction. | Sloths—Fiction. | Building—Fiction.
Classification: LCC PZ7.1.W545 Jc 2020 (print) | LCC PZ7.1.W545 (ebook) | DDC [E]—dc23
Interior design by Nicole Gastonguay
MANUFACTURED IN CHINA
10 9 8 7 6 5 4 3 2 1
First Edition

JASPER & OLLIE
BUILD A FORT

by Alex Willan

Hey, Ollie, what do you want to do today?

Doubleday Books for Young Readers

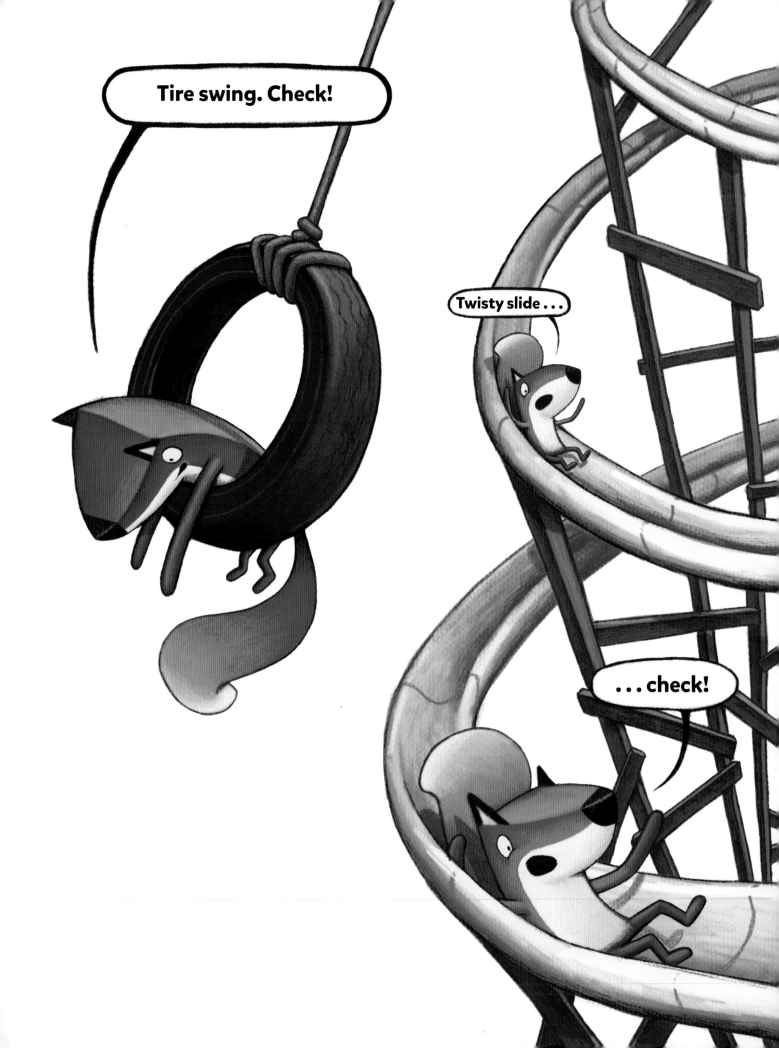

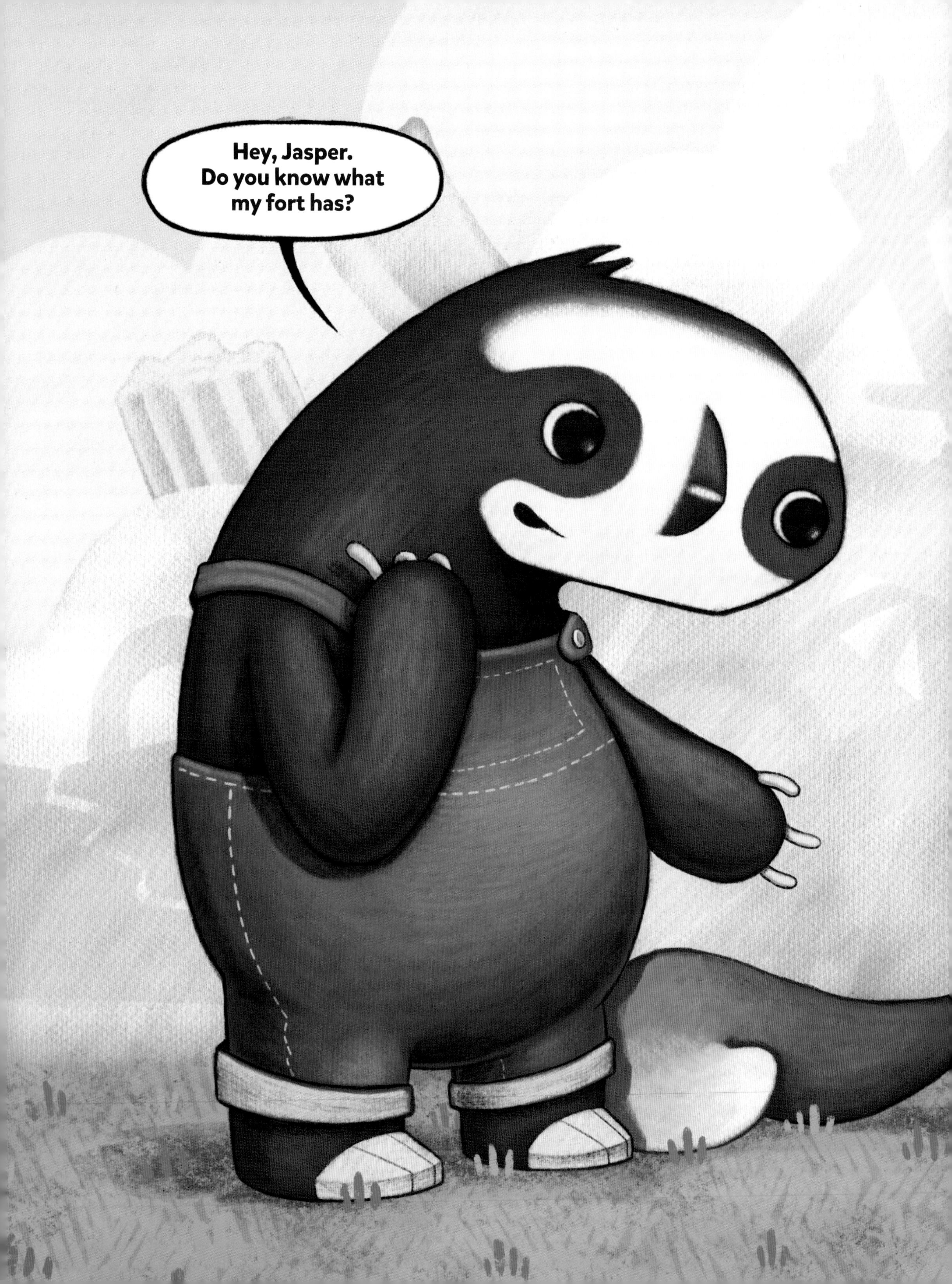
Hey, Jasper. Do you know what my fort has?